Everyone Has A Danger Alarm

Helping Kids Go from Stress to Calm

Kathy Luoma~Bennett

Illustrated by Quinn Elsey

Tellwell Talent
www.tellwell.ca

ISBN
978-0-2288-4677-2 (Paperback)
978-0-2288-4678-9 (eBook)

Preface

Dear parents, caregivers, therapists and helpers,

In this story, children and parents will be introduced to the autonomic nervous system's fight, flight, freeze response. It will help children understand this innate response is automatic and not created by the child.

Using a five-step process, children will learn about and improve their skill in managing challenging reactions. By learning to notice the responses in their body and recognizing these as a signal—a danger alarm—they can then tune down and turn off that alarm with practice and repetition.

I hope you enjoy this story and that it can be another tool to help children self-regulate and increase their resilience.

Dedication

This book is dedicated to all children who have lived trauma and to all children who have struggled with emotion regulation. I wish you and your family healing on your journey. It is my hope that no child ever thinks that they are a bad kid.

I'm a good kid, right?

I don't always feel like a good kid ... especially when my danger alarm goes off.

My danger alarm turns on all by itself.

When my danger alarm goes off,
I can feel like a lion. Roar!!!

I get MAD. I yell. I stomp. I slam.
I feel the fight inside me.

Adults don't like it when I do that.

I don't either. It makes me feel like a bad kid.

When my danger alarm goes off,
I can feel like a cheetah. Whoosh!!!

I get really **SCARED**. I run away. I hide.
I am alone. I feel the flight inside me.

That's my danger alarm too. It tells me that I am scared.

When I run and hide the adults worry that I might get hurt. When I run away the adults worry that I might get lost.

I don't like to upset them. My body feels like it needs to get away.

When my danger alarm goes off,
I can feel like a turtle. Freeze! Don't move!!!

That's my danger alarm again. It is telling me that I am super scared.

When I am frozen and I don't talk, the adults are not sure how to help me feel better. They talk to me and but I can't answer them. I want to, I just can't make the words come out.

I am **SUPER SCARED.** I am frozen to the ground and solid like a rock. I am invisible. I feel the freeze inside me. I can't talk.

I have a danger alarm.

I am not a bad kid.

When the danger alarm in my body notices something scary I fight, or flight or freeze. That's my danger alarm turning on. It does it all by itself. I don't even tell it to!

DANGER!!

My danger alarm says, "Yell, run, hide! You are going to get hurt!"

Sometimes, it's a little alarm and I don't really notice.

My heart starts beating a little faster. Tap, Tap, Tap.

Or I feel a little flutter in my stomach. Flit, flit, flit.

Or my legs feel wiggly and want to run or move. Jitter, Jitter, Jitter.

If I *really* pay attention, I feel those in my body.

Other times, it's a really BIG alarm and everyone notices. I fight, or flight or freeze.

I want to say thank you to my body!

When there is danger you make sure I notice
and turn on my danger alarm.
You want me to be safe!

When you *think* there is danger, you make sure
I notice and turn my danger alarm on.
You want me to be safe!

Everyone has a danger alarm, and that's a really good thing. It's important to notice when there is danger.

But what if my danger alarm goes off a lot?
What if it stays on all the time?

What if my body thinks I am *always* in danger?
My body believes that the world and people are
not safe.

Am I always in danger? Is everyone unsafe?

Yell! I feel the fight inside of me!

Run! I feel the flight inside of me!

Hide! I feel the freeze inside of me!

Sometimes the danger alarm
in my body turns on really fast.

Danger! Danger!

I jump if I hear a loud noise.

Then I find out it was just a balloon popping!

Sometimes people near me will raise their voice. I notice and I wait for something else to happen. Will the noise go away? Is there danger?

Sometimes people can have a scary look on their face and stand big and tall over me. I notice!

Noticing my danger alarm is a really great thing. Then I get to ask: am I safe right now?

I notice scary looks. I notice when someone is big and tall over me. I notice loud voices.

Then I really notice if there is danger right now. Maybe there was danger a long time ago. Is there danger here? With this person? In this moment?

I notice and I look around.

And you know what else?

When my danger alarm turns on I look and listen. Is there danger. When I see there is no danger, I take a deep breath. I sigh. Phew!

I am not in any danger at all.

There is no danger right in front of me,

or behind me,

or beside me.

I am okay!

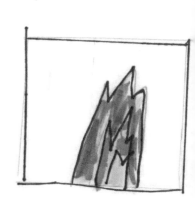

I listen to my alarm if
there is a real danger
like that.

I am starting to notice when my danger alarm goes off.

Is there real danger?

A fire is danger.

Someone who has their arm up ready to hit is danger.

A tornado is danger.

Look. Listen.

"Poof"

I get away from the danger. I can get help from an adult.

What I am learning is that most of the time when my danger alarm goes off, I am not in danger at all. Even when my body feels that I am. Even when my brain thinks I am. I can learn that I am okay.

I am safe and people are safe. There is no one who really wants to hurt me. The world is a safe place. There are lots of people to trust.

When there is no danger, I do not need to fight or flight or freeze.

I am okay. I can turn off my danger alarm.

And did you know we all have the power to turn off our danger alarm?

I am going to share that superpower with you right now.

Look inside your body.

Sometimes you find the danger in your stomach.

Your heart might feel the danger when it beats super fast or super slow.

Your skin might feel the danger when you notice your hands are sweaty.

Your hands might feel the danger. They feel twitchy and your legs are ready to run.

Sometimes it feels little. Sometimes it feels big.

Your brain tells you there is danger too. It listens to your body. And then your body listens to your brain.

Breathe

Look inside your body. Find where the danger alarm is inside of you. When you find it, sit with it.

Keep your attention on it. Notice the shape the color, the size, the feel of your danger alarm.

The more you sit with it, the smaller the danger alarm will get. Stay inside your body. Notice the danger alarm getting smaller. And smaller. And smaller.

It's hard to sit with it, but you can do it! That's your superpower hard at work.

Breathe.

I am so happy you are noticing your danger alarm inside your body!

Breathe. You are okay.

You can tell yourself not to yell, run, or hide.

You can tell your body not to fight or flight or freeze.

There is no danger.

It's okay, danger alarm. Shhhh!

You can say inside your brain, "I am okay. I am safe. There is no danger."

To really make sure you have turned off your danger alarm, breathe three times like this:

Take an In breath.

Then take a Long out breath.

Keep doing that until you feel your body calm on the inside.

Now that you are calm, you can wonder what made your danger alarm go off. Remember that the next time your danger alarm turns on, if there is no danger you can turn your danger alarm off with your superpower.

You are noticing when there really is danger and when there is no danger after all.

So remember to say:

I am okay.

I am safe.

I am loved.

I am not alone.

I will always have people who will love me and take care of me.

Instructions:

Copy down this page to remind you of the five steps to turn off your danger alarm. Remember, it takes practice.

Here are the five steps to turn off your danger alarm:

1. Notice

2. Look

3. Sit

4. Say

5. Breathe

Notice my danger alarm has gone off. (If there is *real* danger get away and get help from an adult.)

I want to run or hide or yell. I am ready to fight or flight or freeze.

Look inside my body to find my danger alarm. Its there, inside my body.

It might be big or little.

Sit inside my body. Stay inside my body with my danger alarm. Breathe.

Say to my danger alarm, "I am okay. I am safe. There is no danger. Shhhhh!"

Breathe in and then breathe out a long out breath. Do this three times.

Manufactured by Amazon.ca
Bolton, ON